1

This book is dedicated to all my friends and family who have supported and encouraged me to continue to dream big and seek excellence.

Jonathan the Elephant Goes 4th

By Andrew W. Merced

Ethan A. Santana

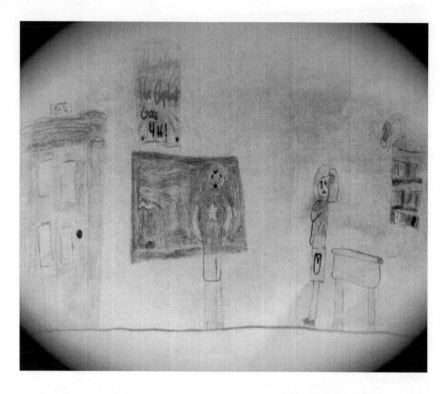

Jonathan was so happy following his normal routine until he found out that Annabelle was putting on a play called Dance of the Blueberries.

"Jonathan would you like to be in my play?" asked Annabelle.

Annabelle gave the script to Jonathan and waited for an answer. Jonathan began to read the script.

"I am not doing this play Annabelle, this play is for babies!" said Jonathan.

Jonathan stomped both his feet and buried his five toes inside his flesh. No one heard the stomp, because Jonathans' spongy flesh always helped him to move silently.

Michael felt the vibrations as he walked
passed Jonathan and his sister.

"He thinks the play is for babies, but the
only one acting like a baby is Jonathan!"
said Annabelle angrily.

Both Michael and Annabelle did not notice that Jonathan had disappeared.

"Let us go look for Jonathan and find out what is really upsetting him?" suggested Michael.

Annabelle shrugged her shoulders as Michael looked at his younger sister and smiled.

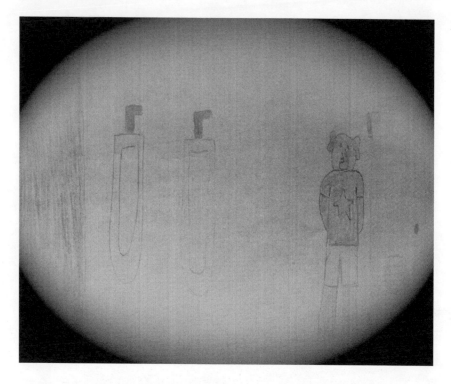

"Annabelle we really need to get to the bottom of this," said Michael.

"Do you know where Jonathan is?" asked Annabelle.

"I think I know where Jonathan may have gone," Michael said.

10

Michael found Jonathan in the school bathroom. Jonathan was hiding behind the door when Michael called out his name. Jonathan pretended that he was not there by not answering, however, Michael noticed his big feet.

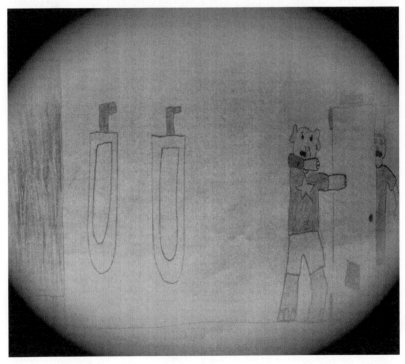

Michael was about to open the door when Jonathan pushed the door open. At that moment he heard a loud "**THUMP!**"

Jonathan did not realize that he had bumped Michael's head against the door and that Michael was hurt.

A classmate by the name of Bluing J. Smith witnessed the whole incident in the bathroom. Bluing could not believe that Jonathan could do such a thing to Michael, because they were the best of friends.

"Michael stay right here I am going to get help," said Bluing.

Bluing told Mrs. Swear the whole story. Mrs. Swear could not believe what she had just heard, because Jonathan was one of her best students. Mrs. Swear knocked on the Boy's bathroom door.

"Michael can you please come out of the bathroom?" asked Mrs. Swear.

Michael explained the whole story to Mrs. Swear who at this point was really upset. Mrs. Swear decided that the school dean needed to handle this matter.

The school dean and the nurse were both notified at the same time along with Jonathans' parents. Jonathan the Elephant sat with his head bent low as the school dean began questioning him.

"Jonathan why did you hurt Michael?" asked the dean.

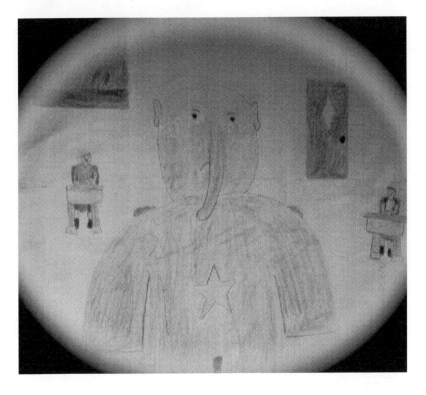

"I was angry and I did not want to be in the school play," replied Jonathan nervously.

"**UGHHH!**" grunted Jonathan angrily.

"The Dance of the Blueberries!" Jonathan shouted.

"Young man settle down and calm down this very instant!" said the dean.

"If you do not calm down and calm yourself I am afraid that your parents will have to come to school," warned the dean.

"I don't want my parents to come to school, but that play gets me so angry," said Jonathan.

"Jonathan even though you have the right to express anger you do not have the right to hurt others," said the dean.

"What you did was unacceptable and not the proper way to handle things," said the school dean.

"You must use your words and speak to someone you trust!" said the dean.

"Jonathan learning how to express your feelings in a positive way will lead to better choices," said the dean.

Jonathan tried to focus on the deans' advice, but he chose to ignore it. In fact he still thought that Annabelle's play would turn him into a baby. Jonathan returned to his classroom and did not speak to anyone. He just sat behind his desk with a grim look upon his face.

The school bell rang and all the students left the classroom, however, Mrs. Swear requested that Jonathan see her at the end of the class.

"I am very disappointed in you," said Mrs. Swear.

"I will need to speak with your parents to see how we can help you," said Mrs. Swear.

"NO!" yelled Jonathan.

"Jonathan, please do not get upset!" requested Mrs. Swear.

"We want to help you understand how to cope with your anger," said his teacher.

Jonathan slowly walked out of the classroom with his head and trunk hung low

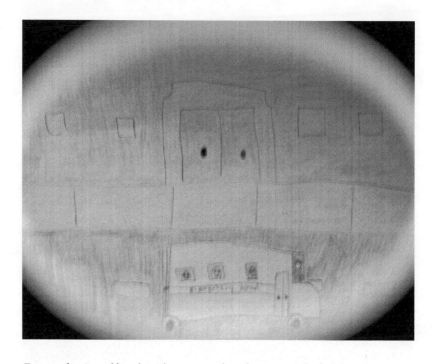

Jonathan climbed onto the bus and felt miserable. He wondered what would his parents say or do once they found out what he had done. Jonathan's heart raced as the bus came to a full stop in front of his house. His knees began to rattle as his removed the seatbelt.

Richie the dog and Wanda the horse were his best friends and they were waiting on the sidewalk.

"Hi Jonathan!" chimed Richie and Wanda.

Jonathan did not reply. He was too ashamed to tell his friends what he had done to Michael. Jonathan slowly inhaled and told Richie what he had done. Richie was so curious.

"Why did you do this?" asked Richie.

Wanda scratched her beautiful brown mane of hair.

"Jonathan teenagers never act this way!" said Wanda.

"You really need to control your anger and start acting your age," said Richie.

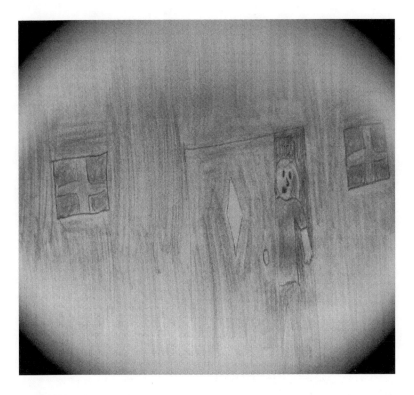

"My advice is for you to apologize to Annabelle and Michael," said the wise Wanda.

Richie and Wanda were in front of Jonathans' home when they were both thinking of ways to help him.

"Jonathan are you ready to go?" asked his mother.

"Where are we going?" wondered Jonathan.

"We are going to Babe Land to buy Aunt Mary Sue a baby gift," said his mother

"But I hate baby stuff!" said Jonathan.

"Of course you do," answered his mother softly.

Babe Land was a very busy store. Richie, Wanda and Jonathan noticed that many people were buying baby items.

"Attention customers don't forget to visit Aisle 3 to get your discount!" said the store clerk.

The store clerk forgot to turn off the speaker when all of sudden a loud baby cry came screeching over the store.

"Forget about your discount in Aisle 3, remove the crying baby from the Aisle immediately!" these were the thoughts in Jonathan's head.

"I can't take this anymore!" yelled Jonathan. "I am going to Aisle 3 and getting rid of the baby items in this store!" Jonathan said angrily.

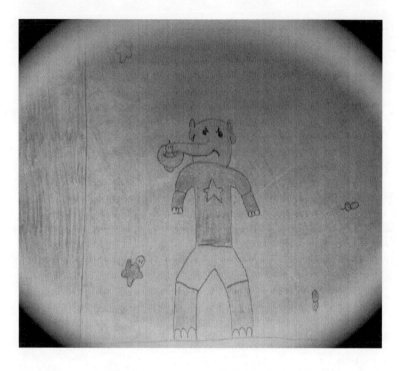

Jonathan quickly ran to Aisle 3 and tossed many toys with his long trunk onto the floor. He ran to the next aisle and repeated the same thing over and over until the shelves in the entire store were empty. Jonathan was about to empty the last aisle when he heard both his friends yell, "**STOP!**"

Richie and Wanda grabbed Jonathans' trunk. "Why are you doing this?" they asked.

"I am trying to get rid of all the baby items in the store!" replied Jonathan.

"That does not make sense!" said Wanda.

An announcement came over the loud speaker once more and this time it was for Jonathan.

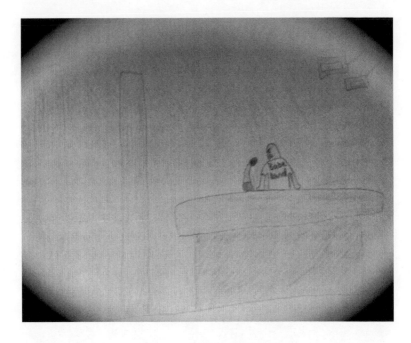

"Will the parent of a grey elephant report to the manager's desk!" said the clerk.

Jonathans' mother could not believe what she was watching on the video screen.

"Jonathan what have you done?" said his mother.

Two security officers approached the desk with the manager of the store.

"Your son must either clean up the entire store or we will have to have the security officers handle this matter!" said the manager.

Jonathan began to clean up the mess that he had made. After he finished he went over to the store manager.

"I am very sorry Sir for messing up your store," said Jonathan.

"I would like to purchase a baby item for my Aunt Mary Sue."

The store manager could see that Jonathan learned his lesson and allowed him to buy the toy.

"Do not worry he will clean this store right this instant!" she said angrily.

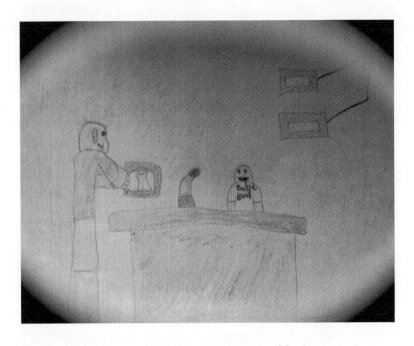

Jonathan came back with a stuffed toy Dalmatian and named him Andy. The toy had long droopy ears, black and white spots with a tag that read Andy. Jonathans' mother was very happy that her son took responsibility for his actions and apologized to the store manager.

"Jonathan I am very proud of you for doing the right thing and facing your fears," said his mother.

Jonathan and his friends left the store with his mother and went to his aunts' house to deliver the gift. All of sudden he heard people shout "**SURPRISE!**"

Jonathan gasped, so this was the surprise all along. His family was giving a surprise baby shower for his Aunt Mary Sue. Annabelle's gift to Aunt Mary Sue was the play Dance of the Blueberries and mother's gift was the baby gift.

Jonathan pulled the toy out of his bag and gave it to his aunt.

"This is for your baby!" smiled Jonathan.

Jonathans' aunt gave him a kiss on his cheek and patted him on his head.

"I know your baby cousin will love it!" said the aunt.

Jonathan spotted Annabelle and Michael across the room and walked straight up to them.

"Annabelle I am so sorry for upsetting you and for not doing the play."

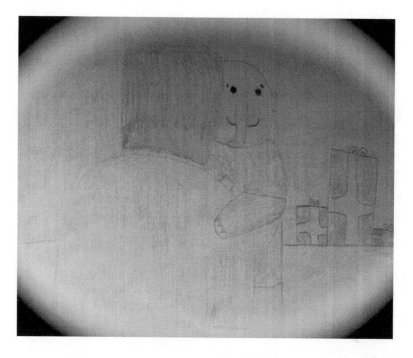

"Michael I am sorry for hurting you, forgive me for acting like a baby," said Jonathan.

Annabelle and Michael both looked at each other.

"Jonathan we forgive you and we love you very much," they said.

They ran up to Jonathan the Elephant and wrapped their arms around him.

"Wow I guess doing the right thing does have good rewards in the end!" said Jonathan.

That is true!" said Wanda.

"Jeremiah 17:10 tells us, "I the Lord search the heart and examine the mind, to reward a man according to his conduct, according to what his deeds deserve."

Jonathan the elephant learned a valuable lesson, if you do the right thing and don't be afraid of doing what is right, you will receive great rewards.

The End

"You have got to keep autistic children engaged with the world. You cannot let them tune out."

Temple Grandin

"Autistics are the ultimate square pegs, and the problem with pounding a square peg into a round hole is not that the hammering is hard work. It's that you're destroying the peg."
—**Paul Collins**, author

"It seems that for success in science or art, a dash of autism is essential"   Hans Asperger.

"Acceptance of difference is more important than achieving normalcy. Tolerance is not good enough because it demands change or at least movement toward an external norm."-Unknown

"Someone with Asperger's really is like you, just more extreme." – Winnie Dunn

"I have autism. It is not a disorder or a disease. IGNORANCE is a disorder AND a disease. IT needs to be eradicated." -Robert Moran

"If you're an underdog, mentally disabled, physically disabled, if you don't fit in, if you're not as pretty as the others, you can still be a hero."
-- Steve Guttenberg

"The only disability in life is a bad attitude."
-- Scott Hamilton

"I choose not to place "DIS", in my ability."
-- Robert M. Hensel

"Disability is a matter of perception. If you can do just one thing well, you're needed by someone."
-- Martina Navratilova

"Life is not measured by the number of breaths we take, but by the moments that take our breath away." - Unknown

"Hard things are put in our way, not to stop us, but to call out our courage and strength." Unknown

"Being disabled should not mean being disqualified from having access to every aspect of life." Emma Thompson

"If we are to achieve a richer culture, we must weave one in which each diverse human gift will find a fitting place." Margaret Meade

Resources for Autism

The Center for Autism

Headquarters:

3905 Ford Road, Suite 6, Philadelphia PA 19131

Northeast Philadelphia:

2801 Grant Avenue, Philadelphia, PA 19114

Administrative Offices:

Monroe Office Building, One Winding Way, Philadelphia PA 19131

Phone: 215.878.3400 / Fax: 215.878.2082 / E-Mail: info@thecenterforautism.org

Autism Now

National Autism Resource & Information Center

1825 K Street NW, Suite 1200

Washington, DC 20006

National Information and Referral Call Center

202.600.3480

Toll Free: 855.8Autism (1.855.828.8476)

Fax: 202 534-3731

E-mail: info@autismnow.org

Top 10 Autism Websites Recommended by Parents

By Maureen Higgins

1. www.autismspeaks.org

 One of the leading autism science and advocacy organizations. Autism Speaks provides a comprehensive resource guide for all states. The site also boasts an impressive list of apps that parents may find useful, including games that focus on communication and social skills.

2. www.autism-society.org

 Another great site that includes helpful resources for those with autism, family members, as well as professionals. Autism Society also gives updates on the latest autism news and press releases.

3. www.disabilityscoop.com

 Sign up for Disability Scoop's e-mail news to receive the most current updates on developmental disabilities. Disability Scoop's experts have been cited by multiple online news sites, including USA Today and People.com.

4. www.autismnj.org

 Run by a network of professionals and parents, Autism New Jersey strives to provide New Jersey residents affected by autism with the most up to date information, including info on Health Care and insurance mandates in New Jersey.

5. www.autism.com

 The Autism Research Institute focuses on researching the causes of autism, as well as developing safe and effective treatments for those currently affected by the disorder.

6. www.autismweb.com

Managed by parents, Autism Web includes great insights on different autism teaching methods. The site also provides a forum where parents can go to share their stories, give updates on their children's progress, and share recipes that may be useful for picky eaters.

7. www.ahany.org

The Asperger Syndrome and High Functioning Autism Association website offers some great resources for those with higher functioning autism. Ahany also provides a great list of summer programs and day camps in New York, as well as useful questions to ask when choosing a camp or summer program for your special needs child.

8. www.autismhwy.com

Started by a woman whose son was diagnosed with autism, Autism Highway is both informative and fun. Easy to navigate, Autism Highway provides an extensive list of Autism related events and specialists. In addition, Autism Highway includes many fun games that children are sure to enjoy!

9. www.autismbeacon.com

Also started by the parent of a child with autism, Autism Beacon strives to supply the best resources for autism treatments. Autism Beacon presents a lengthy range of articles on autism, including sensitive topics such as bullying and sexuality.

10. www.autism.healingthresholds.com

Healing Thresholds includes information on many different therapy treatments for children with autism.

Made in the USA
Lexington, KY
09 January 2015